This story is 100% true.

The only things that have been changed are the characters, the locations and the events.

The Legend of
Old Captain Sue

written & illustrated by

Ian Cartwright

I once heard a story
although I'm not sure it's true,
of a bad greedy pirate
called Old Captain Sue

Known in St. Merryn
to be grumpy and mean,
she wore tatty old clothes
and was not very clean

YE OLDE
PIG
&
HEN

With an old wooden leg
and a hook for a hand,
she'd pretty much failed
at all that she planned

But one last adventure
before she's too old,
there was a rumour going round
of some far away gold

Sue found her old kit
and blew off the dust,
most of the things were
covered in rust

An old map was inside
but it raised many fears,
it seemed that this story
had dated back years

Along with the map was a
compass and shovel,
she hoped to find treasure
without any trouble

She headed out west,
fearless and bold,
to the island of plenty....
or so she was told

Out on the ocean
no spoon or no dish,
she lived on a diet of
black rum and fish

As the days went by
Sue feared the worst,
she started to think that
her mission was cursed

Then a look through the telescope
showed the map to be true,
and put a smile on the face
of old Captain Sue

She stepped on the island
holding the map,
making sure this old tale
wasn't a trap

Following a trail to
X marks the spot,
to search for the treasure
that most had forgot

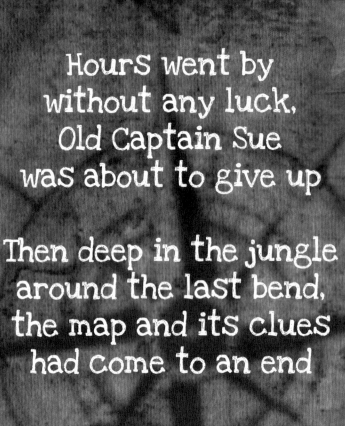

Hours went by
without any luck,
Old Captain Sue
was about to give up

Then deep in the jungle
around the last bend,
the map and its clues
had come to an end

Shark
Bay

Sue dug through the mud,
the rocks and the sand,
blisters and cuts
covered her hand

with one final effort
her spade made a "thud",
on a chest full of treasure
made of rotten old wood

She loaded the booty
onto her boat,
then set sail for England
ready to gloat

"I'm rich! I'm rich! I'm rich!"

"Get in **there** you little **beauty!**"

Halfway back home
the boat gave a shudder,
something was lurking
it knocked off her rudder

A creature she'd heard of
but never once seen,
a big six eyed monster
all slimy and green

It opened it's mouth
and was ready to munch,
the old Cornish pirate was about to be lunch

Its fat green tentacles
flipped up the boat,
and old Captain Sue
slid straight down its throat

She landed inside
the monster's big belly,
it was full of dead fishes,
and awfully smelly

So she took out her cutlass
and chopped at the beast,
she didn't intend to be
a part of it's feast

She shouted
"I wont be staying, but thanks all the same!"
and sliced her way out the same way she came

She swam for her life
and onto dry land,
but like all her adventures
it wasn't as planned

On the world's smallest island
she found herself stuck,
the one legged pirate
was all out of luck!

What happened next
is a little unclear.
Some say she swam homeward
without any fear

But the last thing we heard
(many years later)
from Old Captain Sue,
was a note in a bottle
that washed up in Looe

(it's in Cornwall)

for Finley

Printed in Great Britain
by Amazon